D0478520

DATE DUE

JUL 0 1 2005 AUG 0 8 2005	
AUG 1 8 2005	
SEP 0 8 2005	
OCT 2 8 2005	
JUL 1 6 2009 WITHDRAWN	

BRODART, CO.   Cat. No. 23-221-003

The Tale of
Dog Giovanni

To my parents
Margaret & Herbert

Published by Propeller Press
P.O. Box 729, Fort Collins, Colorado 80522
www.propellerpress.com

Text and illustrations copyright © 2001 by Propeller Press
All rights reserved, including the right to reproduce this book or
portions thereof in any form without written permission of the Publisher.

Publisher's Cataloging-in-Publication Data
Gravdahl, John.
The Tale of Dog Giovanni
Story and pictures by John Gravdahl.
1st ed.
p. cm.

SUMMARY: A boy lives next door to a retired opera singer and his
pet dog, Giovanni. The three are friends, but when the old man dies,
friendship renews and continues between the boy and the dog as they
strive to overcome the loss of the friend who brought
them together in the first place.
Audience: Ages 3-8.
LCCN: 00-190198
ISBN: 0-9678577-9-1
1. Dogs--Juvenile fiction.
2. Friendship--Juvenile fiction.
3. Loss (Psychology)--Juvenile fiction.
4. Bereavement--Psychological aspects--Juvenile fiction.
5. Gardening--Juvenile fiction.
6. Performing arts--Juvenile fiction.
I. Title
PZ7.G7725Tal 2001   [E]
QBI00-901200

Text of this book set in Giovanni book and italic.
Illustrations created with watercolor pencils and gouache.

Printed in Hong Kong
1 3 5 7 9 10 8 6 4 2

The Tale of Dog Giovanni

Story and Pictures by John Gravdahl

Wow! Ow!

How did *this* happen?
I always eat my veggies,
but when I opened my eyes
one morning,
things were sure different.
I had a bad case of polka dots
and spots were all around me.
I was home from school
and lonesome too,
real dullsville until . . .

Leapin' Leafhoppers!?

What's that *fuss* out there?
Stupendous sounds came
bouncing in on the breeze
like pickles on pumpernickel.
My ears popped up
and when I jumped out of bed,
I found a big surprise.

"*Oh solo mio!*"
It was Julius, my friend, at the end of his garden *singing* to a
petunia!
How peculiar! His wild voice was winging in the wind, loud and strong enough to wake everyone in town. And his dog, Giovanni, was right there too, waiting for his turn to woof it up.

My mood improved,
so I wrote a note
and sent out
an airmail message.

"Helloooo Neighbors!"

I hollered out loud
with a perfect pitch . . .

"Morning, Red!"
Julius said, with a wink and
a blink and a smile. *"Looks like
you're a little out of tune today."*
"Not any more,"
I replied, grinning in the window,
*"your songs are **good** medicine.
You should sing for PEOPLE too."*
He laughed when I said that,
and here's why . . .

When Julius was younger
people would hunger
just to hear him sing —
for kings and queens
and lots of normal people too.
He was in the spotlight
all 'round the world and
everywhere he went folks cheered
because they loved him so much.
"Now," he said, *"I just like to
fiddle around in the garden."*

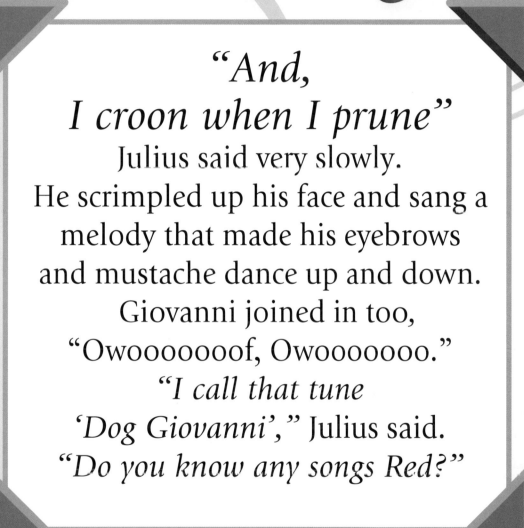

"And,
I croon when I prune"
Julius said very slowly.
He scrimpled up his face and sang a
melody that made his eyebrows
and mustache dance up and down.
Giovanni joined in too,
"Owooooooof, Owooooooo."
"I call that tune
'Dog Giovanni'," Julius said.
"Do you know any songs Red?"

"You bet," I yelped.
"Old MacDonald had a farm,
e i e i o !"
Julius was very impressed,
"HuuuuuuuuWeeeeee Red!
That's mighty fine!
Maybe we can learn some
new ones together sometime."

Next morning at ten,
they were out there again.
"It's 'Opera Time' Red!"
This was a really big show,
with singing and dancing
and acting, *just for me.*
Giovanni jumped up and
hooted a hundred times.
"He forgets the words,"
Julius said, *"but I don't mind.
He's a big ham."*

From that day on,
I was singing a song
all the rest of the year.
Julius waved whenever I ran by.
Some days when I came
home from school, we all sang
operas together in the garden.
"Just dig the music," Julius said,
*"When you sing with zing
it helps everything grow."*

Then, one day at the end of the season Julius went away for a reason I still don't understand. *"Don't worry, I'm just getting recycled."* he said before he left. *"Some of me will dance and sing and fly away, up around the moon, and whatever's left will come back to Earth, pushin' up daisies."* Then he laughed. *"I guess we're ALL gardeners that way."*

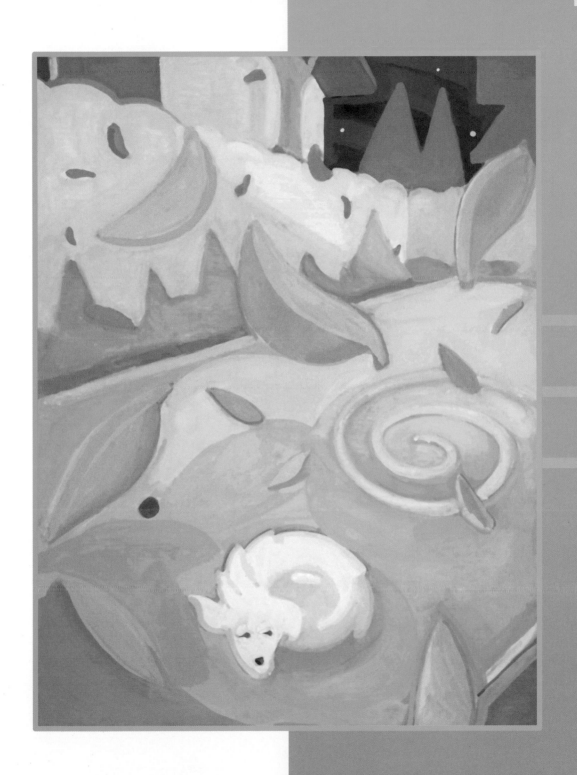

"Good Bye, Julius."

I whispered softly to myself.
I miss him most
when I hum his tunes.
One night, a breeze
carried my voice
up and over to his garden
into the quiet moonlight . . .
where other big ears
were listening . . .

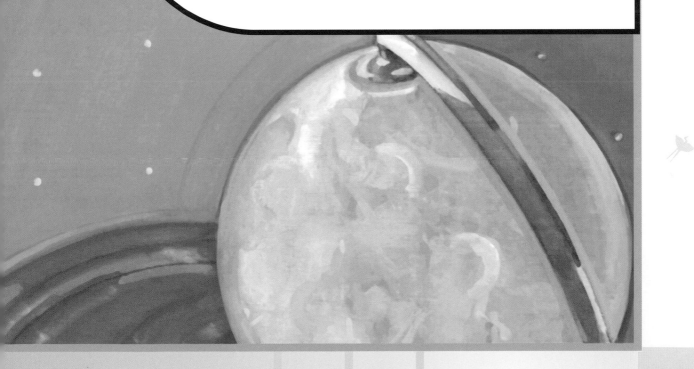

"WOW"

"Bow! Wow! Yowie!"

Giovanni ran up to meet me.
He jumped and woofed and
danced about and ran around
in circles. His tail wagged
so fast I could hardly see it.
We howled with happiness and
my whole face was wet with
tears and *dog kisses!*

Now we're peas in a pod,
growing up together.
And Julius helps us along.
He is near us still when we
remember his happy face and
his big warm voice.
His songs are in our hearts
and they lift us up like wings.
*And every once
in a blue moon . . .*

Giovanni sings!